A DAY BY THE SEA

Barbara Nascimbeni

Today is not like other days. It's an exciting day.

Today we are going to the sea.

"Let's get ready, my FRI-FROU-sweetheart," she says.

HER FAVORITE GLASSES

HER FAVORITE HAT

HER FAVORITE BOOK

MY FAVORITE BOWL

HER BEACH TOWEL

SUNSCREEN

HER SWIMSUIT

HER BEACH UMBRELLA

I'm not FRI-FROU-sweetheart,
I'm FRIDO and she is my owner.

WHEEE

LOLA

"Bye bye Lola! Bye bye Rudi,
see you later, we're going
to the beach."

RUDI

"Look Frido, we're the first
ones here! Let's get settled."

"I'm going to take a quick nap, and then we'll go swimming. Be a good dog and stay here with me," she says.

BOTTLE OF WATER

COOKIES FOR FRIDO

ZZZZZ

BOOK

FRIDO

SUNSCREEN

Of course, I'll be here the whole time...

But when I'm by the sea,
I HAVE to look at the water.

Just for one minute.

So big. I love the sea!

It's wet and cold.

And it's salty!

When I'm by the sea I like to watch the waves coming and going.

GRRRR

WOOF! I'm scaring them.

EEEK!

SPLASH!

Maybe I don't like waves.

When I'm by the sea, it's easy to make friends.

I hope that Lola and Rudi won't be jealous.
I won't tell them.

HOP HOP
HOP HOP

I don't want to share my new friend!

POP

SNIFF

Goodbye, my friend.

Ooh, look at the red goggles!

I can see much better now.

When I'm by the sea
I love to catch some waves.

I'll jump on.

Lola and Rudi will be so proud
of me when I tell them about this.
Watch me! I'm surfing!

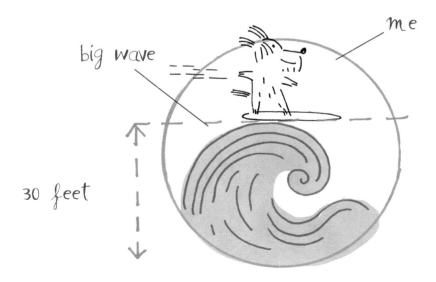

me

big wave

30 feet

Oh no!

Help!

SPLASH

BLOWFISH

PHEW

I can swim!

But yuck, what is that?

MORAY EEL

SEAHORS

BOTTLE

SQUID

JELLYFISH

YUCK

Plastic bottles don't belong in the sea.
I'll pick it up. It should be in the
recycling bin.

OCTOPUS

FLATFISH

When I'm in the sea I can fight against sea monsters!

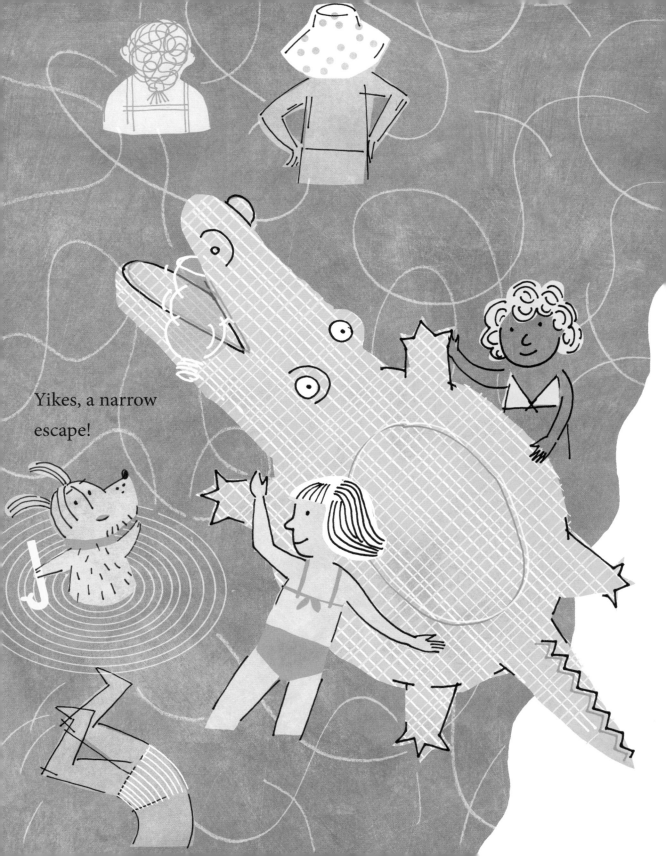

Yikes, a narrow escape!

I should go back, I hope she is still asleep.

"WOW!
You are a great dancer!
Come and practice our new sea dance with us."

When I'm by the sea I can dance really well.

JUMP!

It's time for a photo together! Selfie!

And now some action shots!

CLICK

CLICK

CLICK

POOL

BOAT

DITCH

VOLCANO

When we are by the sea we build the
biggest sandcastle in the world.
It's hard work.

DGE

RAKE

SHOVEL

BUCKET

I must go back to my owner.

"Bye bye! Send me the photos, please!"

DING

DING

But first, ice cream!

ALMOND CRUNCH

ORANGE POPSICLE

FIRECRACKER

CHERRY SUNDAE

ICE CREAM SANDWICH

YUM YUM

When I'm by the sea Vanilla Dream is my favorite!

What? Where did all these
people come from?
How will I find her now?

What's up here?

BIGGEST SANDCASTLE

SCARY SEA MONSTER

ICE CREAM DREAM

YIPPEE

COOL SURFER

NAUGHTY SEAGULL

FRIENDLY DUCK

There she is.
I'm coming right away.

Thank goodness,
she is still asleep.

SHHH,
TIPTOE TIPTOE!
SQUISH

FRIDO

I was here the whole time.

SPLISH SPLASH

"Wake up Frido, let's go swimming."

More swimming?
But I'm exhausted…

YAWN

When I'm by the sea she doesn't
have to know that I like…

to make new friends,

to surf,

to swim with the fish,

to fight against sea monsters,

to do a sea dance,

to take photos with friends,

to build a sandcastle,

and that I love Vanilla Dream ice cream…

When we are by the sea, she knows that her FRI-FROU-sweetheart is the sweetest and most well-behaved of all dogs!

For my mother and for my father

A Day by the Sea © 2022 Thames & Hudson Ltd, London
Text and Illustrations © 2022 Barbara Nascimbeni

Copyedited by Ruth Redford

First published in the United States of America in 2022 by
Thames & Hudson Inc., 500 Fifth Avenue, New York, New York 10110

ISBN 978-0-500-65295-4

Library of Congress Control Number 2021944029

Printed and bound in China by C&C Offset Printing Co. Ltd

Be the first to know about our new releases,
exclusive content and author events by visiting
thamesandhudson.com
thamesandhudsonusa.com
thamesandhudson.com.au